KaNgaroo
aNd the Crew

Mary Elizabeth Salzmann

Consulting Editor, Diane Craig, M.A./Reading Specialist

ABDO
Publishing Company

Published by ABDO Publishing Company, 4940 Viking Drive, Edina, Minnesota 55435.

Printed in the United States.

Credits
Edited by: Pam Price
Curriculum Coordinator: Nancy Tuminelly
Cover and Interior Design and Production: Mighty Media
Photo and Illustration Credits: BananaStock Ltd., Corbis Images, Digital Vision, Hemera, Tracy Kompelien, PhotoDisc

Library of Congress Cataloging-in-Publication Data

Salzmann, Mary Elizabeth, 1968-
    Kangaroo and the crew / Mary Elizabeth Salzmann.
        p. cm. -- (Rhyme time)
    Includes index.
    ISBN 1-59197-797-5 (hardcover)
    ISBN 1-59197-903-X (paperback)
    1. English language--Rhyme--Juvenile literature. I. Title. II. Rhyme time (ABDO Publishing Company)

    PE1517.S3535 2004
    428.1'3--dc22
                                                                    2004050404

SandCastle™ books are created by a professional team of educators, reading specialists, and content developers around five essential components that include phonemic awareness, phonics, vocabulary, text comprehension, and fluency. All books are written, reviewed, and leveled for guided reading, early intervention reading, and Accelerated Reader® programs and designed for use in shared, guided, and independent reading and writing activities to support a balanced approach to literacy instruction.

Let Us Know

After reading the book, SandCastle would like you to tell us your stories about reading. What is your favorite page? Was there something hard that you needed help with? Share the ups and downs of learning to read. We want to hear from you! To get posted on the ABDO Publishing Company Web site, send us e-mail at:

sandcastle@abdopub.com

SandCastle Level: Transitional

Words that rhyme do not have to be spelled the same. These words rhyme with each other:

blue

kangaroo

canoe

moo

stew

clue

crew   view

dew

zoo

Jenna and Andrea's swimming suits are **blue**.

Iris and Ken ride with their parents in a **canoe**.

Adam's hair is very short.
This style is called a **crew** cut.

Gabriella lost her favorite CD.

She doesn't have a **clue** where it could be.

The flower is covered with dew.

The kangaroo carries her baby in a special pouch on her stomach.

Rosa's mom helps her chop
vegetables to make **stew**.

Eddie and Molly pet the calf.

They laugh when it says **moo**.

Bryan uses binoculars to enjoy the **view**.

Steve and Alan learn about snakes at the **zoo**.

Kangaroo and the Crew

Kangaroo was part of a crew.

The crew made plans to go to the zoo.

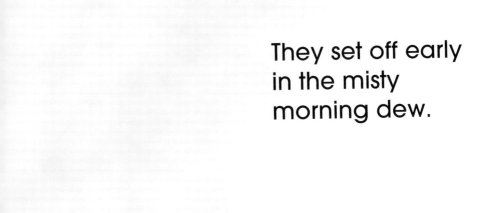

They set off early
in the misty
morning dew.

They were lost until they came to a sign that was blue.

On the sign was printed a clue.

ZOO

The clue led them to a canoe.
They paddled until the zoo
came in to view.

"Yahoo!
We made it to the zoo," said Kangaroo.
Cow said, "Moo!"
Rooster said, "Cock-a-doodle-doo!"

After touring the zoo,
they went home and had some stew.

Rhyming Riddle

What do you call the people who paddle a small boat that has pointed ends?

Canoe crew

Glossary

binoculars. a magnifying device you look through with both eyes to get a better look as things that are far away

calf. the young offspring of a large mammal, such as a cow, elephant, giraffe, whale, or seal

clue. a piece of information that helps you find an answer or a solution

dew. moisture that collects on cool surfaces, usually at night

stew. a dish made with meat or fish and vegetables that is cooked slowly

About SandCastle™

A professional team of educators, reading specialists, and content developers created the SandCastle™ series to support young readers as they develop reading skills and strategies and increase their general knowledge. The SandCastle™ series has four levels that correspond to early literacy development in young children. The levels are provided to help teachers and parents select the appropriate books for young readers.

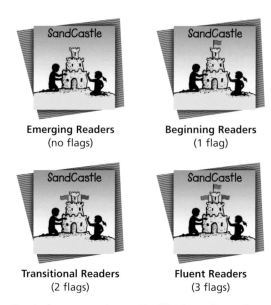

Emerging Readers
(no flags)

Beginning Readers
(1 flag)

Transitional Readers
(2 flags)

Fluent Readers
(3 flags)

These levels are meant only as a guide. All levels are subject to change.

To see a complete list of SandCastle™ books and other nonfiction titles from ABDO Publishing Company, visit www.abdopub.com or contact us at:
4940 Viking Drive, Edina, Minnesota 55435 • 1-800-800-1312 • fax: 1-952-831-1632